Blondie

Rapunzel's Royal Pony

For Halina —T.R.

randomhousekids.com

ISBN 978-0-7364-3267-2 (trade)
ISBN 978-0-7364-8164-9 (lib. bdg.)

Printed in the United States of America
10 9 8 7 6 5 4 3 2 1

Blondie

Rapunzel's Royal Pony

By Tennant Redbank

Illustrated by the Disney Storybook Art Team

Random House 🏠 New York

"All set," Rapunzel said as she finished brushing Blondie's mane. She added one last purple flower. "Now you're the cutest pony I know!"

Blondie swung her mane back and forth. She knew the flowers looked cute. She had peeked at herself in the water trough. She neighed happily.

"You like it," Rapunzel said. "Right?"

Blondie let out a soft whinny.

Rapunzel kissed her on the nose. "Just wait," she said. "I have a big surprise for you. Soon!" She danced off toward the palace.

A surprise?

Blondie loved surprises!

Maybe it was a new saddle! Maybe it was gold horseshoes! Maybe it was honey oats—her favorite treat!

"I wonder what it is," Blondie said.

"I know," Summer said. "I heard the king talking about it."

Summer had been waiting for Blondie by her stall. She was a kitten, and Blondie's best friend at the palace. They had become Rapunzel's pets around the same time.

"So?" Blondie asked. "What's the surprise?"

"Rapunzel is getting another palace pet!" Summer told her.

"Oh." Blondie lowered her head. *But why?*

Rapunzel already had Blondie and Summer. There was Meadow the skunk, too. Why did she need another pet?

"Aren't you happy?" Summer asked. "Another pet means another friend!"

"I guess," Blondie said.

Blondie hadn't always been one of Rapunzel's pets. Once upon a time, she was just a little horse with a big dream. She had wanted to be a royal horse. But the other horses told her she was too small.

One day, Blondie had sneaked into a palace parade. Then she tripped on her mane. She stumbled right in front of Rapunzel!

Rapunzel went to her. She wasn't mad.

She just braided Blondie's mane so she wouldn't trip again.

After the parade, Rapunzel took the little pony to the palace. From then on, Blondie was Rapunzel's special pony.

"What do you think the new pet is?" Blondie asked.

"I hope it's another kitten," Summer said. She began licking her paws.

"I hope it's not another pony!" Blondie said.

"Maybe it will be a bunny," Summer said excitedly. "Or a fox. Or a baby deer. Wouldn't any of those be nice?"

Blondie shook her head. "No," she said. Bunnies, foxes, and baby deer were worse than another pony. They were likely to be very cute! Rapunzel might spend all her time with something that cute!

"Why are you worried?" Summer asked. "You and I arrived around the same time and became good friends right away. And when Meadow came, we all got along fine."

"That's different," Blondie said. "We were all new back then, and equally cute." Then she had an idea. "I can't count on just being cute," she told Summer. "I have to show Rapunzel that I'm helpful, too!"

Summer stopped licking her paws. She looked up.

"Helpful?" she asked.

"Yes!" Blondie said. "I have a plan!"

Blondie galloped to the garden. She knew exactly how to be helpful!

Rapunzel loved flowers, like the pretty one she had put in Blondie's mane! But picking flowers took time. And Rapunzel was so busy. Blondie would pick some for her!

Blondie skidded to a stop outside the garden walls. She peeked inside. The

garden was one of the most beautiful places at the palace. Red and pink petunias grew in neat rows by the stone walls. Purple lilacs hung from a wooden trellis. Wild daisies lined the path. In the center was a pool with a white marble fountain. Pink water lilies floated on the surface.

The water lilies caught Blondie's eye. They were perfect for Rapunzel's hair! She pranced over to the fountain.

A lily pad the size of a dinner plate floated just out of her reach. On it was a pretty pink bloom. Blondie put her hooves on the edge of the pool and leaned forward. She couldn't . . . quite . . . reach.

She stretched her neck farther.

She reached with her nose, and then . . .

SPLASH!

A geyser of water shot up. Blondie jumped back. It still soaked her, nose to tail.

Blondie shook herself off. What had happened?

A large green toad sat laughing at the edge of the pool. He must have splashed her when he jumped into the water right in front of her!

Blondie laughed, too. "I guess that's *your* lily pad, Mr. Toad," she said. "All right. I'll leave it alone. Rapunzel likes lilacs just as much as she likes lilies!"

Blondie trotted over to the lilac bush. Now that she thought about it, lilacs were better anyway. Rapunzel would love their purple petals. Blondie broke off a cluster of lilacs. Then she plucked some more. She looked at her bouquet. It was pretty, but it needed something else.

Blondie looked around. There, beyond a low iron fence, were the biggest, most beautiful pink petunias.

Blondie picked the three best ones. Then she saw a basket on the ground next to the petunias. What luck!

Blondie put all the petunias in the basket and trotted off to show Rapunzel. The princess would love how helpful Blondie was. She'd forget all about needing a new pet!

Blondie headed toward the courtyard. Rapunzel spent a lot of time there. She had grown up locked in a tower, so now she stayed outside as much as she could.

And there she was! Rapunzel was painting a picture. Pascal the chameleon was with her. He had been Rapunzel's friend for a long, long time.

Blondie pranced over to Rapunzel. She laid the basket at Rapunzel's feet. She tossed her mane.

"What's this?" Rapunzel asked. "Blondie, did you bring me flowers? Thank you!"

"Well done," Pascal told Blondie. Rapunzel couldn't understand him, but Blondie could. She flushed with pride. Pascal didn't give praise very often.

"These are lovely!" Rapunzel said. She pulled out one flower after another.

"Purple lilacs. Pink—" Rapunzel stopped. She looked at the pink petunia more closely. "Oh, oh, uh-oh."

Blondie tilted her head. What was wrong?

Rapunzel gulped. "Blondie, you and I might be in trouble." She held out the pink petunias. "These are the gardener's prize petunias. She was going to enter them in the flower show tomorrow!"

"Pascal, what am I going to do?" Blondie asked.

Rapunzel had run off to talk to the gardener to smooth things over. Blondie felt awful.

"I just wanted Rapunzel to see how helpful I am," Blondie said. "A new palace pet is on the way. I don't want Rapunzel to forget me." She let out a small sigh.

Pascal shook his head. "Don't be silly," he said. "Rapunzel loves you. And she'll love you just as much when she gets a new pet."

"Really?" Blondie asked.

"Of course!" Pascal said. "For years, I was Rapunzel's only animal friend. Then she got you and Summer. And Meadow came later, remember?"

Blondie nodded.

"And she loves us all," Pascal said. He turned and climbed over the palace wall.

Blondie felt a little better. She sat down. But after a minute, she got up. She paced the courtyard. She loved them all because they were all different. But what if Rapunzel got another pony? Blondie was the only pony!

Pascal had told her not to worry. But she couldn't help it. The flowers had been a bad idea. She could still find another way to be helpful!

What could she do?

Rapunzel's painting caught her eye. It was a picture of the bay around the castle.

Blondie looked at it closely. It wasn't done yet. Then she noticed something else. Rapunzel was almost out of blue

paint. She would need more to finish. Water meant she needed a lot of blue.

Blondie could make more!

She imagined how happy Rapunzel would be. Blondie had never made paint before. But she had watched Rapunzel do it many times. She could figure it out.

She sat down to think. What was blue?

The sky was blue. But Blondie couldn't make paint from the sky. Water was blue. Sometimes Pascal was blue. What else was blue?

Huckleberries!

That was it! Huckleberries would be

perfect for making blue paint!

Blondie knew about a huckleberry bush not far away. It was next to the stables. All the horses ate from it. Unlike the petunias, it was nobody's prize plant. Blondie could take all the berries she needed.

She hurried to the bush. She picked a whole bucket of huckleberries. Then she carted them to the courtyard.

Rapunzel wasn't back yet. *Good,* Blondie thought.

Blondie found an empty barrel in the corner of the courtyard and tipped the

huckleberries into it. Then she poured in some linseed oil. It was hard to hold the slippery glass bottle in her teeth! She added water and dropped in an egg. That was how Rapunzel made paint.

Blondie jumped into the barrel. She stomped the berries with her hooves. They squished. They squashed. They were mashed up with the oil and water and egg.

Soon the barrel was full of blue paint. Hooray!

Blondie leaped out of the barrel. She couldn't wait to show Rapunzel!

Blondie raced across the courtyard. She climbed the palace steps and neighed loudly.

"Blondie?" she heard Rapunzel call. "Is that you? What's going on?"

Rapunzel came out the palace door. She stood at the top of the steps. Her hand flew to her mouth. Then she started to laugh.

"Is that—? Is that blue paint?" she asked.

Blondie nodded. But how did Rapunzel know? She had left the barrel of paint back in the courtyard!

Blondie turned to look behind her.

Uh-oh.

A trail of blue hoofprints led down the stairs and across the courtyard.

Blondie caught a glimpse of her own tail and her braided mane. They were blue, too.

Blondie had just wanted to make some paint. Instead she had painted the courtyard—and herself—blue!

Blondie hung her head. She sighed. Behind her, people had immediately started washing the stairs and the courtyard. They had even started washing her.

Her tail took forever to clean.

Blondie was worried about Rapunzel. Rapunzel had laughed. She had even thanked Blondie for making the paint. But Blondie knew she hadn't really been

helpful. She had just made more work for others. And she'd had to take an extra bath, too!

Blondie moped back to the stables. She would stay there. No more trying to help! She only made things worse.

Blondie lay down in her stall. She chewed a little hay. She thought about the new pet.

"It must be another pony," she said. "One with spots. I bet its mane is twice as long as mine. And its tail is twice as curly. I bet the new pony can make paint, no problem. And pick the right flowers."

Blondie was feeling very sorry for herself. Then she heard footsteps. They walked up to the stables.

"Maximus?" a voice called.

Blondie knew that voice. It was Flynn's.

Flynn had helped Rapunzel escape from the tower. On the way, he had become good friends with the horse Maximus. They were both very strong and brave. Blondie sat up to listen.

"Hey, boy," Flynn said. "I have a job for us."

Blondie peeked under the stall door. Flynn was giving Maximus an apple.

Maximus crunched it noisily.

Mmm. Blondie really loved apples! Her mouth watered.

Flynn kept talking. "I've heard reports of trouble outside the village," he said.

Trouble? Blondie pricked up her ears.

"It's a band of thugs," Flynn said. "They've been spooking cows, stealing eggs, and fleecing sheep. Can you help me?"

Blondie jumped to her feet. She almost shouted, "Yes!" Luckily, she remembered that Flynn wasn't talking to *her*.

Maximus neighed.

"Good," Flynn said. "I know Rapunzel will be glad."

Of course! This was how Blondie could help Rapunzel. She would go with Flynn and Maximus. She would help capture the thugs!

Blondie narrowed her eyes. She had a feeling she should sneak out. Maximus and Flynn might not let her come.

She heard Flynn take out Maximus's saddle. She heard the jangle of the reins.

She peeked again. Flynn jumped onto Maximus's back. They left the stable.

Very quietly, Blondie followed them.

Flynn and Maximus didn't go fast. They stopped often. They were sneaking along, looking for clues.

Flynn talked to farmers. He asked questions. Maximus sniffed the ground. He chatted with the local cows and horses.

Finally, they got a lead. The thugs were at a nearby barn!

Flynn and Maximus raced off.

"Wait!" Blondie yelled. Maximus didn't

hear her. She ran as fast as she could, but her legs were much shorter than Maximus's.

Blondie made it to the old barn. Flynn and Maximus were outside, plotting. Flynn drew a plan in the dirt.

Blondie trotted over to them.

Flynn glanced at her and his mouth dropped open in shock.

"Blondie?" Maximus said. "What are you doing here?"

"I'm going to help you!" Blondie said. "I'm going to round up the thugs! Then Rapunzel won't need another palace pet!"

Flynn shook his head. He couldn't understand what Blondie was saying. But he knew one thing. "Oh, no," he said. "No way. No ponies! Not going to happen. Nuh-uh."

"He's right," said Maximus. "You should stay here." *CRASH!*

A loud noise came from inside the barn.

"We need to hurry!" Blondie said. "The thugs are going to get away!"

Flynn grabbed a big stick from the ground. He nodded at Maximus. "Okay, Max," he said. "Let's go. You stay here, Blondie."

Flynn kicked in the door. He leaped through it, waving the stick. Maximus was right behind him. He pawed the ground. Blondie brought up the rear. She whipped her mane from side to side. She wasn't going to stay behind!

The barn was full of thugs. Big, mean, nasty thugs. Blondie shivered. They were scary! But she would do anything to help Rapunzel.

The thugs turned as the door crashed open. They stared at the three intruders. One of the thugs was about ten feet tall. One had horns on his helmet. Another

had a hook for a hand. Blondie gulped.

"Wait a second," Flynn said. He lowered the stick. "I know you guys! You're the thugs from the Snuggly Duckling!"

"We know you, too," said the thug with the hook. He picked Flynn up and dangled him by his left leg.

Blondie backed away. *Oh, no!* What should she do? Flynn was in trouble!

Then she felt a paw on her shoulder. She jumped.

It was a dog! A hairy thug dog! With big, mean . . .

Oh! Blondie thought. The thug dog was only a puppy. And she looked kind of nice. She had pretty golden fur.

The thug dog smiled at Blondie. "Don't worry," she said. "They're just teasing him."

"They are?" Blondie asked.

"Sure," she said. "My name is Daisy."

"I'm Blondie." Daisy and Blondie touched noses.

"There. See?" Daisy waved a paw at the center of the barn. The thugs were tossing Flynn back and forth like a ball.

"Guys?" Flynn called. "Guys, put me down? I didn't know it was you! I heard talk of spooking cows. And fleecing sheep. And stealing eggs!"

The thugs dropped Flynn . . . on his head.

"Attila needed milk and eggs for his cupcakes," the thug with the hook explained. "And Bruiser needed wool. He likes to knit. We left money to pay for them."

"Want to try?" Attila asked. He held out a tray of pink frosted cupcakes.

"Don't mind if I do," Flynn said. He took one.

"So the thugs aren't bad guys?" Blondie asked Daisy.

Daisy shook her head. "Nope," she said. "They're friends of the princess. They helped her, once upon a time."

Part of Blondie was relieved. But part of her was sad. This had been her last chance to show Rapunzel how helpful she was. But she hadn't been helpful at all.

"Want to play hide-and-seek?" Daisy asked. Blondie cheered up right away. She loved hide-and-seek! Summer never wanted to play. Pascal was too good at it. And Meadow was easy to find. Her skunk scent gave her away.

"Okay!" Blondie said. "You're it!"

After hide-and-seek, Flynn, Maximus, Blondie, and Daisy ate pink cupcakes. They sang show tunes. They watched a mime and admired one thug's collection of tiny glass unicorns.

Blondie said goodbye to her new friend. She would miss her! Then they headed home.

"That was some adventure, hey,

Blondie?" Flynn said. He gave her a wink.

Blondie neighed. Flynn was riding Maximus. Blondie was trotting after them. She felt like part of the team now.

Maximus led them back to the village. They passed meadows and streams and lots of trees. The castle was just across the bay.

Blondie was happy to be going back. But she felt sad, too. She had wanted to show Rapunzel she was helpful.

She had tried her best. She had picked flowers for Rapunzel. She had made paint. She had even tracked down thugs.

But nothing had gone quite right.

Soon Rapunzel would have a new pet.
Soon she would forget all about Blondie!

Maximus, Flynn, and Blondie crossed
the bridge. Someone was running toward
them. It was Rapunzel.

All Rapunzel could reach was Flynn's
leg. She shook it. "I was so worried about
you!" she said. "I can't believe you left
without telling me!"

She gave Maximus a pat. "Thank you
for taking care of him, Maximus," she
said sweetly.

Then Rapunzel knelt beside Blondie.

Blondie bowed her head. "And you? You ran off, too! I had no idea where you were. You're so brave! But please don't scare me like that again."

Blondie looked up at her.

"I didn't forget your surprise," Rapunzel said.

Blondie sighed. She hadn't forgotten about the surprise, either. The new pet was all she had thought about lately.

Rapunzel got to her feet. She shaded her eyes and looked across the bridge. "I think it's coming now."

Blondie heard hoofbeats. She saw a

horse and rider coming toward her. It was a big horse with a huge rider. The rider wore a helmet. The helmet had two long, curving horns.

It was one of the thugs from the barn!

"Hello, Vladimir," Rapunzel said.

"I have your present," Vladimir said. "Thanks for letting us keep her a little longer. Gunther wanted to finish his new painting of her." Vladimir reached under his tunic and pulled out—

"A puppy!" Rapunzel said. "Thank you so much!"

Vladimir leaned down and placed the

golden puppy in her arms. Blondie could hardly watch.

Wait a second. . . .

A golden puppy?

Daisy?

Daisy was Rapunzel's new pet?

That changed everything!

Daisy was great! Blondie imagined all the good times they would have together.

Blondie pranced over to Daisy. "Hello, friend!" she said.

Daisy wagged her tail. "Hi, Blondie!" She gave her pony friend a big wet puppy lick on the nose.

Blondie smiled. Summer was right. Pascal was right. A new pet wasn't something to worry about. A new pet meant a new friend. It didn't matter how many friends Blondie already had. She could always welcome one more!

Each Palace Pet has a story

Cinderella

Pumpkin

Snow White

Berry

Aurora

Beauty

to tell—collect them all!

Belle

Teacup

Tiana

Bayou

Ariel

Treasure